W9-ANT-356

Miriam at the River

For Barbara Diamond Goldin who walks and talks the mystery.

For Malerie Yolen Cohen who lives on the path .

For Elizabeth Harding Gold who tends the flame.

And for the memory of Isabelle Berlin Yolen, may her name be for a blessing.

—J.Y.

KAR-BEN PUBLISHING, INC.
An imprint of Lerner Publishing Group, Inc.
241 First Avenue North
Minneapolis, MN 55401 USA
1-800-4-KARBEN

Website address: www.karben.com

Main body text set in **Caecilia LT Std.**
Typeface provided by **Adobe Systems.**

Library of Congress Cataloging-in-Publication Data

Names: Yolen, Jane, author. | Le, Khoa, 1982– illustrator.
Title: Miriam at the river / Jane Yolen ; illustrated by Khoa Le.
Description: Minneapolis, MN : Kar-Ben Publishing, [2020] | Series: Bible | Summary: Seven-year-old Miriam places her baby brother's basket in the Nile River, watches the Pharoah's daughter draw him out and name him Moses, and ponders a vision of other water parting. Includes note on the biblical story on which this is based.
Identifiers: LCCN 2019007491| ISBN 9781541544000 (lb : alk. paper) | ISBN 9781541544017 (pb : alk. paper)
Subjects: LCSH: Miriam (Biblical figure)—Juvenile fiction. | Moses (Biblical leader)—Juvenile fiction. | CYAC: Miriam (Biblical figure)—Fiction. | Moses (Biblical leader)—Fiction. | Jews—History—To 1200 B.C.—Fiction. | Egypt—Civilization—To 332 B.C.—Fiction. | Bible stories—Old Testament.
Classification: LCC PZ7.Y78 Mj 2020 | DDC [E]—dc23

LC record available at https://lccn.loc.gov/2019007491

Manufactured in the United States of America
1-45431-39686-5/21/2019

MIRIAM at the RIVER

JANE YOLEN

ILLUSTRATIONS BY KHOA LE

I creep to the riverside
in the soft dark of night's end.
In a woven Basket lies my little brother,
so young, he does not even have a name.
He sleeps, and in his dreams
his legs and arms move
as if he is swimming.

I am afraid and not afraid.
I am only seven years old.
We are slaves in Egypt
and in Egypt, Pharaoh's words
and Pharaoh's laws
must be obeyed,
even the wicked ones.
But God's law is what I follow.
And God's voice is the one I hear,
even when others do not listen
to what God has to say.

We go to the Nile before the sun rises.
For now it is just a red line,
spilling along the horizon.

I look up the water and down,
then to the hiding place I have chosen.
Sedge, bulrush, papyrus, reeds,
all I need to hide my brother
from the Pharaoh's men,
and hide me from prying Egyptian eyes.

I say a quick blessing over him,
for he is so small, so much at risk.
I give him a sister's kiss.
Once again I look around.
Then I place the basket in the river
near the bending reeds.
The basket is heavy and I am small.
I pretend I am simply a child
playing by the waterside.
But under my robe, my heart
beats so loudly, I am certain
anyone near will hear.

One quick push
and the basket sails
towards the middle of the reeds
where the water is coolest.
Mother has woven the basket so tightly,
it does not sink, but skips
over little schools of fish,
glossy as silver bangles.
Then the sun comes out
and the bangles turn the color
of Pharaoh's jewels.

The basket skims past a yellow-billed stork
who stands with angel wings held high.
Past an ibis dipping its long beak into the water
so very like a scribe's pen in ink.

Past a hippopotamus
wallowing in the small tide
of the basket's passing.

The Nile's water ripples,
then parts on either side of the basket.
Suddenly, in my mind,
I see another water parting:
fiercer, higher, a great wall of it.
What water is this? I wonder,
for it is surely not the Nile.
I could ask God for an answer,
though often God's answers are not clear.
Father says prophecy is a cloudy glass,
a muddy river, a curtain pulled a bit aside.

But I ask God anyway.
Like a soft breeze,
that comforts in the middle
of an Egyptian summer,
God whispers in my ear,
"Your little brother is in my care
till he comes home."
But where is home? I wonder.
Then, taking a deep breath,
I accept that answer,
leaving my brother to be rocked
in the river's arms.
Then I whisk my footprints away
so there can be no blame.
Sometimes courage comes
from what you do,
sometimes from what you do *not* do.

Now I hide near a palm tree,
sitting on my heels to wait.
All that I've dreamed,
all that I've seen in my mind's eye,
depends on the Pharaoh's daughter.
I hope she is not too late.
There are crocodiles in the river.
There is fate.

And here she comes,
a young woman to bathe
in the waters of the Nile.
She is tall, slim, dark, beautiful.
She has no child of her own.
She will hear a baby's cry,
draw him from the river.
She will be mother to a slave,
who will capture her heart,
until another water parts.

She commands her handmaidens
to pull the basket from the reeds.
She picks the baby out of his water cradle.
"I shall call him Moses,"
she tells her servants,
"for he was drawn from the water."

I sneak away,
quiet as a whisper.
That is the story I will tell my parents.
And with it, for now,
we shall be content
till some day all the world
will know my brother's name.

Where This Story Comes From

In the biblical story of Exodus and in later tales from the Midrash*, we learn about Miriam the prophet. We first meet seven-year-old Miriam with her infant brother at the Nile River. It is the first of three of the most important times of her life. Each time after this, Miriam will lend him her courage and strength and her gift of prophecy when his own are not enough. Each time water is involved.

First, as a child herself, she hides him in a basket that floats on the Nile River until Pharaoh's daughter draws him out, names him Moses, and brings him to the palace as her own. Moses' real mother becomes his nursemaid.

Second, Moses grows up as an Egyptian prince. He makes his way to Midian where he marries and has sons. He hears God ordering him from a burning bush to return to Egypt. Miriam greets him on his return and, with him, leads the Jews from Egypt. As they flee from soldiers in chariots, they come to the Red Sea which parts—that great wall of water Miriam had seen in her prophecy. Once the Hebrews are across, the waters quickly close.

Third, forced to wander for forty years in the desert where Moses brings the stone tablets with the Ten Commandments down from the mountaintop, God sends down manna, a food, for them to eat, and provides a rock from which water gushes—"Miriam's well."

Three waters—the Nile River, the Red Sea, and the well that follows Miriam, giving water at her command. This story of the Jewish people starts with the brave little girl and her infant brother at the river.

*A midrash is an interpretation or commentary that reflects on Torah text.